To my sons and daughters, who showed me how
the camaraderie of skateboarding transcends stereotypes
and prejudices, Nyree, Tyreek, Nasir, Nia, and Tiffani.
Love you!

- A NOTE FROM FRANK -

It took a month of rolling down a hill into a pile of rocks . . . repeatedly falling and crashing around a half pipe, for me—at age thirty-nine—to give up any dreams of becoming even an average skateboarder.

My children, who watched at the bottom of hills and on the sides of ramps, were amused. I found myself thinking about a phrase as I sat patiently on a curb, while my daughter stuck Band-Aids on my knee.

"Let me show you how we used to do it."

A phrase used by fathers daily had a very different meaning now. My children are now showing me how it's done. One kickflip at a time. Show-offs.

When painting this story, I chose my signature style of mannerism. It seamlessly portrays the wicked moves and tricks I've seen my children and their friends perform over the years by capturing the energy and essence of these moves, rather than the physical reality of them. I couldn't imagine another style capturing the high-flying acrobatics through the air, up walls, and down ramps.

The urban settings drenched in graffiti backgrounds can be any city. The transformed font reminds me of how a simple plumbing pipe becomes a skateboarder's instrument—gliding over it like Duke Ellington sliding his fingers over the piano keys.

With this story, I wanted to show kids that their interests don't need to be confined by any expectations. I hope readers enjoy the story and are encouraged to follow their own unique talents.

Be you, be great.

BLOOMSBURY CHILDREN'S BOOKS
Bloomsbury Publishing Inc., part of Bloomsbury Publishing Plc
1385 Broadway, New York, NY 10018

BLOOMSBURY, BLOOMSBURY CHILDREN'S BOOKS, and the Diana logo are trademarks of Bloomsbury Publishing Plc

First published in the United States of America in March 2022
by Bloomsbury Children's Books

Library of Congress Cataloging-in-Publication Data
Names: Morrison, Frank, author, illustrator.
Title: Kick push / by Frank Morrison.
Description: New York : Bloomsbury, 2022.
Summary: When Epic's family moves to a new neighborhood, he has a hard time making friends
and fitting in with his skateboard, but the trick to making new friends is to be yourself!
Identifiers: LCCN 2021026248 (print) | LCCN 2021026249 (e-book) |
ISBN 978-1-5476-0592-7 (hardcover) • ISBN 978-1-5476-0593-4 (e-book) • ISBN 978-1-5476-0594-1 (e-PDF)
Subjects: CYAC: Skateboarding–Fiction. | Friendship–Fiction. |Self-acceptance–Fiction. | Moving, Household–Fiction.
Classification: LCC PZ7.1.M6729 Ki 2022 (print) | LCC PZ7.1.M6729 (e-book) | DDC [E]–dc23
LC record available at https://lccn.loc.gov/2021026248
LC e-book record available at https://lccn.loc.gov/2021026249

Typeset in Burbank Small • Book design by Yelena Safronova
Printed and bound in China by Leo Paper Products, Heshan, Guangdong
2 4 6 8 10 9 7 5 3 1

To find out more about our authors and books visit www.bloomsbury.com and sign up for our newsletters.

Kick Push

Frank Morrison

BLOOMSBURY
CHILDREN'S BOOKS
NEW YORK LONDON OXFORD NEW DELHI SYDNEY

MEET IVAN, the kickflipping, big rail king.
He's been grinding the streets with moves so big,
his friends call him EPIC.

A new day in a new neighborhood?
No sweat.

These streets might be different,
but Epic's tricks are the same.

KiCK
PUSH
PLOP!

What's the point of gnarly tricks
without compadres to cheer 'em?

Why be Epic if no one can see?

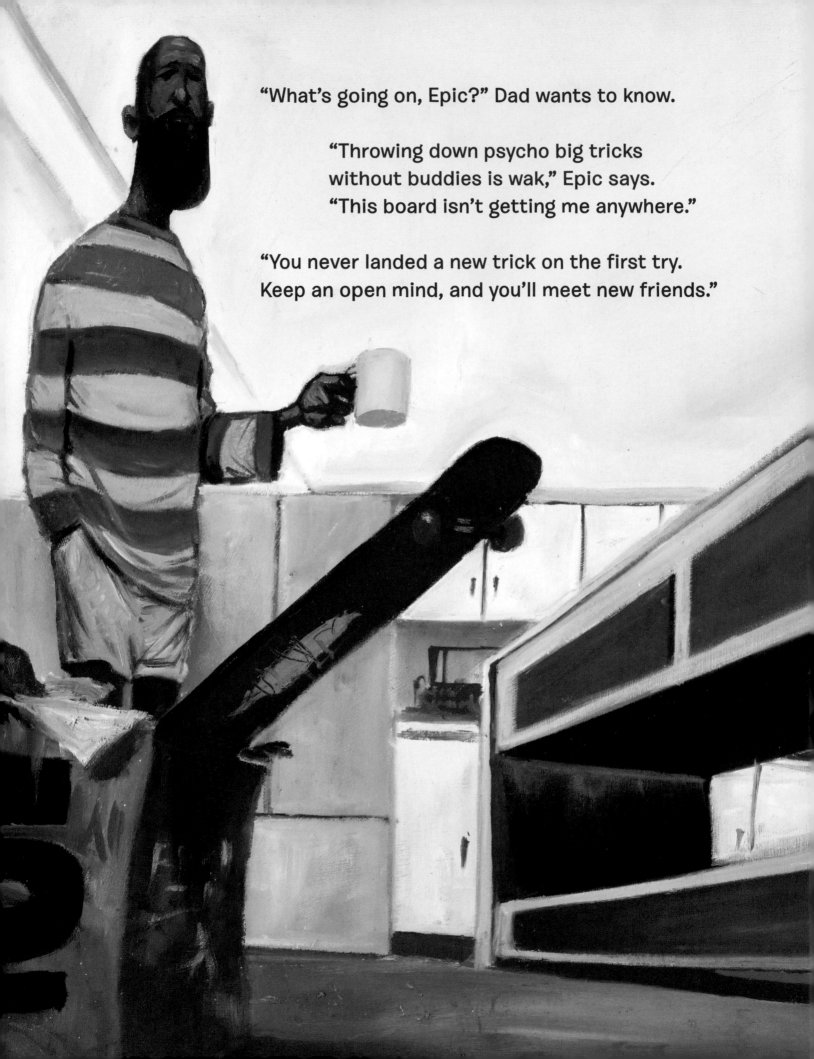

"What's going on, Epic?" Dad wants to know.

"Throwing down psycho big tricks
without buddies is wak," Epic says.
"This board isn't getting me anywhere."

"You never landed a new trick on the first try.
Keep an open mind, and you'll meet new friends."

KiCK

PUSH

GOODNiGHT.

Epic dragged hisself to bed,
then counted backside flips
to fall sleep.

Defeated and dazed, confused and drenched,
Epic was **not feeling it**.

Epic told his parents about one painful moment after another.

"Sugar, how about you run down to the bodega and treat yourself?" said Momma.

Epic flew past Dad, flipped his board on the banister, slid down to the sidewalk, then disappeared down the block.

KICK

PUSH

KICK

He did a backside fakie on the fire hydrant . . .

KICK
PUSH
FLIP

Landed it!

Epic wove in and out of a sidewalk pickup game . . .

BOUNCE, KA-CLONK, BOUNCE, KA-CLONK!

Epic shimmied past Tiff's House, kickflippin' while the girls did their sidesteppin'.

KICK
PUSH
WOOSH

With the bodega in sight, Epic spotted a rail bigger than any he'd ever attempted . . .

KiCK
PUSH
CLANG

He mongo-footed, then flipped into a switch stance. Took a breath and screeched across the stairs into a 50-50 grind to the bottom, landing in front of the Be Fly Barbershop.

"Like I said . . . **No sweat.**"

Epic hopped inside the bodega and grabbed his favorite snack.

"Are those your friends?" asked the clerk.

"Sick moves, bro!"

"We saw you, we feel you."

"Let's get a session on!" said Epic.

KiCK

PUSH

KiCK!

Away they went.

Back home they started up a gnarly game of Skate.
Back and forth they went until the sun went down.

New neighborhood, new crew,
and even some sweet
new tricks? No doubt.

**BEING YOU IS
PRETTY EPIC.**